Yummers!

JAMES MARSHALL

HOUGHTON MIFFLIN COMPANY BOSTON

Library of Congress Catalog Card Number 72-5400
Printed in the United States of America

RNF ISBN 0-395-14757-3
PAP ISBN 0-395-39590-9

WOZ 20 19 18 17 16 15 14

For Lillian and Cynthia

Emily Pig was upset.

She was gaining weight

and she didn't know why.

"Maybe I should get more

exercise," she said to herself.

The next day Emily jumped rope.

"I don't really like this," she
said, huffing and puffing.

"I have a better idea," said her
best friend, Eugene. "Why don't
you come for a nice long stroll
with me? Walking is the best
exercise of all."

Emily was delighted.

"Walking is more fun," she said.

"It doesn't seem like exercise."

"And there are so many lovely things to see," said Eugene.

But walking made Emily hungry.

"Do you think we have time for a little snack?" she asked.

Eugene knew where to get the most
delicious sandwiches.

"Oh, yummers," said Emily, "all my
favorites. But which one should I
choose?"

"Have more than one," said Eugene.

"I don't want to make a pig of myself,"
said Emily. "I'll just have a tuna fish
and a jelly delight."

"That sounds sensible," said Eugene.

But the sandwiches only made Emily
hungrier.

"Oh, yummers!" she squealed when she
saw the corn-on-the-cob stand.

And what pig can resist corn on the
cob?

The corn was especially tasty, but

very soon Emily's nose began to twitch.

"What is that wonderful smell?" she asked.

"It's coming from Granner's Tea Room,"

said Eugene.

"Granner would never forgive us if we didn't

pop in to say hello," said Emily.

Granner's Tea Room was cozy indeed.

"The scones were scrumptious. Another

platter of scones, please," Emily called.

"And lots of hot butter and jam."

Eugene was still nibbling on his first scone.

"I'm afraid you didn't get enough to eat, Eugene,"
said Emily.

"Yes, I did," answered Eugene. "My scone was very
good."

But Emily was not satisfied.

"Oh, look!" she squealed. "Eskimo pies!"

Eugene didn't particularly like eskimo pies.

But Emily did. She ate three in a row.

As a special treat Eugene purchased a box
of Girl Scout cookies.

"Yummers," said Emily.

But everybody knows that Girl Scout cookies
are even better with milk.

"Let's have a glass of milk with our cookies
at the drugstore," said Emily.

"Nice idea," said Eugene.

But inside the drugstore Emily couldn't help
ordering a vanilla malt, a banana split, and
a small dish of peach ice cream.

"This is simply yummers," she said.

Eugene sipped a glass of skimmed milk.

Leaving the drugstore, Eugene snapped his fingers.

"I almost forgot. This morning I drank the last of my jasmine tea.

Do you mind stopping at the supermarket?"

"Certainly not," replied Emily.

While Eugene was waiting in line, Emily discovered the

free pizza.

"It's so important to sample new products," she said.

In the park, Emily felt awful.

"I have a tummy ache," she moaned.

She could barely finish her cherry pop and
candied apple.

Eugene took Emily home in a taxi.

He was very concerned.

The next morning Eugene paid a call on
his sick friend. But Emily was feeling
much better.

"What do you suppose was the matter?"
asked Eugene.

"It must have been all that walking,"
replied his friend.

Eugene smiled. "Maybe you should stay in
bed and eat plenty of good food."

"Oh, yummers," said Emily.

DATE DUE			

15870

E
MAR

Marshall, James.

Yummers!

NEWPORT ELEMENTARY LIBRARY